my little treasury

Best-Loved
Children's
Stories

Cover illustrated by Jacqueline East
Table of contents illustrated by Margie Moore

Customer Service: 1-800-595-8484 or customer_service@pilbooks.com

www.pilbooks.com

p i kids is a trademark of Publications International, Ltd.,
and is registered in the United States.

8 7 6 5 4 3 2 1

Manufactured in China.

ISBN-13: 978-1-4508-5842-7

my little treasury

Best-Loved
Children's
Stories

 publications international, ltd.

Contents

The Ant and the Grasshopper

Adapted by Catherine McCafferty
Illustrated by Jason Wolff

ummer had just begun. Animals and insects scurried about, enjoying the summer sun. "Summer's here! The best time of the year!" the Grasshopper sang.

A line of ants marched past, carrying bits of food. As they walked along, some crumbs fell. Before the ants could pick up the food, the Grasshopper had eaten it up.

The ant at the end of the line walked up to the Grasshopper.

"We've worked hard to gather this food," said the Ant. "You should have helped us."

"That's what's wrong with your summer song," the Grasshopper sang. "Summertime is for play, not work."

"Summertime is for getting all the food we will need for the winter," said the Ant.

"Winter is far away, I'd rather go and play," said the Grasshopper, turning away.

"Wait!" cried the Ant. "What about the food you took from us?"

The Grasshopper pointed toward a field. "There's a whole field of wheat to replace your crumbs," he called, heading off to a nearby cornfield.

The Grasshopper quickly forgot about the Ant and leaped onto a cornstalk, where soft leaves gave him a shady bed.

"Those ants can work and store. I choose to snooze and snore." He fell fast asleep.

Meanwhile, the Ant lined the tunnels of his home with food and seeds. "When the snow is on the ground, we will be full and warm in our nest," thought the Ant.

All that summer, the Grasshopper trailed the ants, eating his fill of the food they found and resting while they worked to store it.

Then one day, the Grasshopper heard a loud noise. The farmer was harvesting the corn! "I just lost my bed and food!" he cried.

A line of ants was marching past and heard the Grasshopper. The Ant stopped. "The days are getting shorter, my friend," he said. "But there is still time for you to store food and find a winter shelter."

"Not today, I've got to play," sang the Grasshopper, hopping through the grass.

He came across a promising spot under the shade of an old oak tree. But as soon as he had gotten comfortable, he heard a plop!

"Oh, I'm sorry," exclaimed a squirrel in the tree above him. "I'm collecting acorns for the winter. The more the better!"

As the Grasshopper soon saw, the field was filled with squirrels gathering nuts.

The squirrels chattered to one another, "Have you heard? This winter is going to be very snowy!"

All this work was making it very hard to play, and to sleep. The Grasshopper hopped through the field and came across a warm, sunny rock. He was just settling down when the ants began marching by.

"You again!" he said to the Ant. "I was sure that by now you'd have enough. You can't eat all that stuff!"

"It's always better to have a little extra than not enough," the Ant called.

The Grasshopper frowned. The sun had moved, and the rock was now cold.

The Grasshopper hopped off to the apple orchard and found a few small apples on the ground. He munched on them until he was full. Then he settled in for a nap near the root of the tree. The Grasshopper shivered. The sun had already set. "Someone needs to tell the sun that its working day is not done," he sang unhappily.

The sun was one thing the Grasshopper didn't mind seeing at work. With each day, though, it seemed to work less and less.

The ground seemed colder, too. One day, when the Grasshopper tried to nibble an apple, he found that it was frozen. "I don't like my apple in ice," said the Grasshopper.

He was so chilly that it was hard for him to think of a second line to his rhyme. "Ice, nice, rice, mice...."

Then he thought, "Maybe I'll visit my friends, the mice." The Grasshopper crept into the home of the field mouse family, where it was so nice and warm inside.

"Thank you for visiting," said Mother Mouse. "I would invite you to stay, but all of my sisters and brothers are moving in for the winter. Isn't that wonderful? Oh, here they are now!"

A crowd of mice rushed into the nest. The Grasshopper was out of luck at the Mouse house.

The Grasshopper hopped back to the orchard. The ground was so cold that it hurt his tiny feet. "Where are those ants, now that I need them?" sang the Grasshopper.

Suddenly snow began to fall. He had to get inside or he would freeze! Hopping as fast as he could, the Grasshopper raced to the Ant's home. "Is anybody home?" he called.

"Why aren't you out playing in the snow?" asked the wise Ant.

The Grasshopper wanted to say he was just visiting. But he could feel the cold wind on his back. Sadly, the Grasshopper sang, "I should have listened to what you said. Now I'm cold and scared and unfed."

It wasn't his best song, but he hoped the Ant would understand.

He did. But he wanted to be sure that the Grasshopper understood, too. "We got our food for the winter by working hard. If you stay with us, you'll have to work hard, too."

The Grasshopper gulped. But then he remembered the ice and snow.

"Your job will be to sing for us," laughed the Ant. "Because winter is our time to play!"

All that winter, the Grasshopper sang for the Ant and his family. And the next summer, the Grasshopper sang a song as he helped to gather food. "Summer work is slow and steady. When winter comes, I will be ready!"

The City Mouse and the Country Mouse

Adapted by Lisa Harkrader
Illustrated by Dominic Catalano

nce upon a time a country mouse named Oliver lived in a hole under the root of a big, old oak tree. He loved the smell of rich dirt and hearty grass all around him.

One fine fall day Oliver decided to invite his city cousin, Alistair, for a visit.

When Alistair arrived, he set his leather suitcase down and remarked, "I say, cousin, is this your cellar?"

"No," replied Oliver, "it's my home."

Oliver showed Alistair the back of the hole, where he stored his grain. He led his cousin up onto the knob of the old oak root, where he sometimes sat to watch the sunset. Then he sat Alistair down at the tuna-can table and served him a dinner of barleycorn and wheat germ.

Alistair nibbled his meal politely. "This certainly tastes as though it's good for me." He coughed and swallowed. "A bit dry, though, perhaps. Could I bother you for a cup of tea?"

Oliver brewed up a thimble of dandelion tea for them both. "Here's to my cousin Alistair! Thanks for visiting," toasted Oliver.

Oliver awoke early the next morning, as usual. A robin family twittered in the old oak tree. A rooster crowed at a nearby farm.

Alistair squeezed his pillow over his ear. "Oh, dear. What is that confounded racket?" he mumbled.

"That's the sound of morning in the country," said Oliver cheerfully.

Alistair pulled the pillow from his face and opened one eye. "You start your day in the morning?" he asked.

"Here in the country we rise at dawn," Oliver said. "We'd better start the chores."

Alistair reluctantly pulled on a pair of overalls and followed his cousin outside.

While Oliver set to work, Alistair leaned against the root of the old oak tree. After some time, Oliver returned with corn, rye, and acorns, which he piled neatly.

"Thank goodness you're done," Alistair said, collapsing into a wheelbarrow.

Oliver giggled. "We still have lots to do."

Alistair sighed. "I'm simply not cut out for the country life," he said. "A mouse could starve to death here. Come home with me for a while. I'll show you the good life."

Alistair packed his silk pajamas into his fine leather suitcase. Oliver packed his long johns into his beat-up carpetbag. The two mice set out for Alistair's home in the city.

Oliver followed Alistair over fields and valleys, into dark, noisy subway tunnels, and through crowded city streets, until they reached the luxury hotel where Alistair lived.

Oliver stared up at the revolving glass door in front of him. "H-h-how do we get inside, Alistair?"

"Wait till the opening comes around, then run through," Alistair replied. The door swung around, and Alistair swiftly disappeared inside. It took a few more spins before Oliver gave it a try.

Oliver followed Alistair across the beautifully decorated lobby and through a small crack in the wall.

"My apartment," Alistair said when they were inside.

Oliver looked around in amazement. His cousin's home was filled with crystal goblets and linen napkins. The little apartment was lovely, but so different from Oliver's home in the old oak tree.

"We're under the bandstand," Alistair pointed out. "An orchestra plays, and people dance every night until dawn."

"How can you sleep with all the noise?" asked Oliver.

"I sleep during the day," said Alistair. "We do some things a little differently here. Dinner, for example. Follow me!"

Alistair led Oliver through the dining room. They hid behind potted plants and raced under tablecloths. They waited until the chef went to check something in the dining room, then scampered across the kitchen and into the dark pantry.

They climbed up the shelves to the hors d'oeuvres. Alistair gobbled fancy crackers, nibbled pasta, and even managed to chew a hole in a tin of smoked salmon.

"Now this," said Alistair, patting his tummy, "is fine dining."

But all of the hiding and scurrying had scared Oliver. He barely ate a crumb. Alistair was too excited for the next course to notice.

"Tonight the chef is preparing roast duck with herbed potatoes," Alistair said, his mouth watering with anticipation.

Alistair began gathering up bits of food. He didn't notice the chef marching back into the kitchen.

But the chef noticed Alistair. "You again!" he shouted, chasing the mice with a broom.

Alistair and Oliver escaped through a hole under the sink.

"Don't worry," said Alistair. "We'll make up for the measly dinner with dessert."

Alistair showed Oliver the dessert cart. Oliver timidly nibbled the edge of a flaky cream puff. He leaned forward, and *splat!*

A waiter had bumped the cart, and now Oliver was facedown in the cream puff.

Oliver wobbled off the cart. "I'm not cut out for life in the city," he said. "You take too many risks for your dinner. A mouse could starve to death here, too. I'm going home to the good life."

So Oliver dragged his carpetbag back through crowded city streets, over fields and valleys until he reached his hole under the root of the big, old oak tree.

Back at his hotel, Alistair curled up in his bed and listened to the orchestra play.

Both mice sighed. "I love being home," they said.

The Brave Little Tailor

Adapted by Jennifer Boudart
Illustrated by Jeremy Tugeau

ne morning, a little tailor sat in his shop. Suddenly the tailor had a taste for raspberry jelly. He took out a loaf of bread and cut a big slice from it, licking his lips as he spread on some jelly.

The tailor wanted to sew a little bit more before his snack. When he looked up again, a swarm of flies was buzzing around his jelly.

The little man waved the flies away with his hand, but they flew right back.

The tailor grabbed a scrap of cloth and growled, "Now I'll let you have it!" The cloth whooshed as he beat at the buzzing flies.

When he had finished, seven flies lay dead on the table. "The whole world should know of my skill!" said the tailor. He cut a belt just his size. With his finest thread, he sewed the words "Seven in one blow!"

He tied the belt around his waist and shouted, "I feel the need for an adventure!"

The tailor looked for something useful to take with him, but all he found was an old piece of cheese. He put it in his pocket. As he locked the door, he heard a rustle in the bush. A bird was trapped among the thorns.

The tailor gently pulled the bird from the brush. He put it in his pocket with the cheese. Then he set off to find his adventure.

The tailor walked through town and up a mountain. At the top, he met a giant. "Hello, Giant," said the tailor with a bow. "I am on a big adventure. Will you join me?"

"Me, join a little man like you?" rumbled the giant. For an answer, the tailor showed the giant his belt. The giant read the words stitched there: "Seven in one blow!"

The giant, who wasn't too smart, thought that the belt meant seven men, not flies. He found it very hard to believe that this tiny tailor could kill seven men with one blow.

The giant decided to test the little man's strength. "You must be very strong," he said. "Can you do this?" He picked up a stone and squeezed until water dripped from his hand.

The tailor was not as strong as the giant, but he was much more clever. He pulled the cheese from his pocket and squeezed until liquid ran from his palm.

"Well, can you do this?" the giant asked. He picked up another stone and tossed it high into the air. It flew almost out of sight.

"Watch this," the tailor said as he took something else from his pocket. It was the bird, of course, which the tailor sent flying. Pretty soon the bird was out of sight!

This didn't convince the giant. "If you're so strong, help me move this tree," he asked.

The tailor quickly came up with a plan. He walked to the leafy end and said, "I'll carry the heavy branches. It is no trouble for one who can kill seven in one blow."

The giant lifted the tree trunk onto his shoulder. The tailor hopped into the branches and let the giant do all the work. When the giant stopped to rest, the tailor jumped out and pretended to be carrying the leafy end.

"You must be exhausted!" the giant said, a gleam in his eye. He insisted on taking the tailor to his cave to rest. The other giants were sitting down to eat when they arrived.

After dinner, the giant said, "You can sleep here," and pointed to a giant-size bed.

The tailor was a bit suspicious, so he hid in a corner. He watched the giants pound the bed with heavy clubs. They believed they had finally taken care of the pesky tailor.

In the morning, the giants swam in the river. When the tailor appeared, they were so afraid, they ran away without their clothes! The tailor laughed and left the giants behind. Along the road he met some soldiers. One saw the tailor's belt and decided to bring him to meet their king. The king was pleased, and hired the tailor for his army. He also gave him a bag full of gold.

But the other soldiers were jealous. "We will leave your army if we don't get a bag full of gold, too," they told the king.

The king could not lose his army. He decided to get rid of the tailor. "Go kill two giants living in my woods. Your reward will be my daughter's hand and half my land."

The tailor knew this was his chance to become a hero. This was adventure, all right!

The next morning, the tailor rode off to find the giants. "Stay behind until I call you," he told the soldiers who had come with him.

The tailor found the two giants asleep under a tree. He climbed the tree and began dropping acorns on one giant's head.

The giant awoke and turned to the other. "Why did you wake me by thumping my head?" roared the first giant.

Before the second could answer, the angry first giant threw an acorn at him. The two giants fought each other until both fell. The king's soldiers were amazed at what the brave little tailor had done.

"Two giants are easy," said the tailor. "Try seven in one blow."

The king was impressed, but he had one more task. "Bring me a unicorn," he asked.

The tailor soon found one. In fact, it was running straight for him! At the very last second, the tailor jumped out of the way.

He had been standing in front of a tree, and the unicorn's horn stuck into the wood. The tailor rode the unicorn back.

The king had no choice but to keep his promise. He could not prove that the man who married his daughter and took half his kingdom wasn't anything but a hero.

The tailor almost gave up his secret one night, though. In his sleep, he said, "This new fabric will make a fine waistcoat."

His wife leaped from the bed, listening closely. But, awakened by the movement, he cleverly continued, "A man who can kill seven with one blow should have the finest waistcoat around. Right?"

Saint George and the Dragon

Adapted by Brian Conway
Illustrated by Tammie Speer Lyon

his is the tale of Saint George, an orphan who had been raised by fairies. Under their guidance, he grew up brave, calm, strong, courteous, quick, and clever. They taught him to be a noble knight.

At last the time came when George was old enough to seek his destiny. The queen of the fairies called him to see her.

"Your journey starts today," she told him. "You have many adventures before you."

"Yes, Your Majesty," George bowed.

"Always remember one thing," added the queen, tapping George's silver battle helmet. "Your greatest weapon is your mind."

With those words, George set off. He traveled through many wonderful kingdoms. But as George approached the town of Silene, he noticed the land change from lush and green to dark and desolate. There was no grass, only thick mud. It seemed the ground had been crossed by fire. The trees were bare and black, and a foul stench filled the air.

As George walked through this stark land, he did not see a soul—not a bird, not a squirrel, and certainly not a single person.

Soon George saw a castle enclosed by a high wall. When he got closer, George saw a young lady creep quietly through the gate.

"Excuse me," he called politely after her.

"Quiet!" she hushed him. "Leave now if you value your life."

"But I am a brave knight here to help you," George whispered.

"Alas, sir," the woman replied, "you are but one man. I fear that you cannot help."

George looked her in the eyes. "It is my destiny," he said. "I will not go until I have done all I can, even if it costs me my life."

"I am Princess Sabra," she finally said. "Come with me."

Sabra then explained why the kingdom lived in such fear.

A ferocious dragon had ravaged the land. Many men had tried to slay the dragon, but without success. The whole kingdom had moved inside the castle walls for protection.

But soon the dragon ran out of food.

"If you do not feed me sheep each day," the dragon had roared, "I will come through those walls for my breakfast!" So every day, the people provided food for the dragon.

"We gave up our last two sheep this very morning," said Sabra sadly. "Tomorrow we shall have nothing to give the dragon, and we shall all perish."

"Then I have arrived at just the right time," said George bravely.

They soon came to a cave. "To slay the dragon," Sabra told George, "we need help."

In this cave there lived a wise old hermit. When they arrived, he did not turn to look, but spoke as if he knew they were coming.

Long ago, it was told,
Two brave knights would come to know,
The only way to save the rest:
The Serpent's weakness is in his breath.

With that, an ancient hourglass appeared at their feet. George did not understand. He asked the strange little man, but the hermit would speak no more.

When George and Sabra left the cave, it was already dark. They hurried to the sleeping dragon's lair.

As they traveled, George remembered what the queen had said. His best weapon, she had told him, was his mind. He studied the hourglass closely. Each bit of sand looked like a magic crystal frozen in time.

They arrived at the lake. George and Sabra walked softly through the fog so they would not be heard. The sands in the hourglass dropped with every careful step.

"The hourglass will lead us," George whispered. "We must wait until all the sand has dropped through."

The smell as they approached the lair was horrible. George and Sabra watched the icy blue sands drop as the dragon snored.

Suddenly, the dragon stirred. With the blue sands still making their way through the hourglass, he raised up and rubbed his slimy eyes.

Just as the very last grain of sand was dropping through the hourglass, the dragon yawned a great, fiery yawn.

"Now, George!" Sabra shouted.

George knew what to do. He threw the magic hourglass up into the dragon's yawning mouth. It shattered on the dragon's slithering tongue in a cloud of icy mist.

The dragon reared back to hurl a fiery
blast at George and Sabra. But, as fortune
would have it, only cool ice and soft snow
came from the dragon's mouth.

The hermit's magic had transformed
the dragon! His mouth shut tight with ice,
a once-fearsome dragon jumped into the
deep, warm lake. Only there could he keep
from freezing from the inside out.

That dragon never bothered another soul.
Some say they have seen him coming up
for air on occasion, but only on very warm
nights. The dragon would not dare stay
out of the warm water too long, for fear of
becoming a giant icy statue.

George and Sabra had saved the
kingdom. The two arrived at the castle to
great cries of joy and triumph. The grateful
people of Silene were no longer prisoners in
their own kingdom.

The king offered George all he had in
thanks, but George wanted no payment.

"I have many adventures left," George
told the people. "They are my reward."

George continued on his journeys,
sharing his tale along the way. People
everywhere learned of his courage and
selflessness. That is how George, the brave
knight from the land of the fairies, earned
his sainthood.

The Golden Goose

Adapted by Brian Conway
Illustrated by Karen Dugan

 here once was a gentle boy called Samuel. He lived near the forest with his family, who often treated him poorly.

One day Samuel's eldest brother went to cut wood. Their mother packed sweet cake and cider for his trip. In the woods, Samuel's brother came upon a little gray man.

The man said, "Will you share your meal with a tired old man?"

But Samuel's selfish brother refused.

The brother began to chop a tree. After a few strong swings, his ax slipped and cut him. He hurried home to dress his wound.

Now the second brother was called to get the firewood. Their mother also gave him sweet cake and cider for his journey. Before long the second brother also met the old man in the woods.

The man bid him good day and said, "Would you share your meal with a tired old man? I am very hungry and thirsty."

This middle brother was as selfish as the first. "If I give you my food and drink, I won't have enough for myself," he said. "Now get out of my way!"

The second brother walked away and found a tree to chop. But the head of the ax broke off and fell firmly on the brother's foot, and he, too, could no longer work. Samuel's second brother hobbled home.

Samuel said, "I'll cut the wood, Father."

"You know nothing about it," his father replied harshly. "But if you are so willing to get hurt, then go."

Samuel's mother handed him some stale bread and a jug of warm water. In the forest, Samuel met the little gray man as well.

The old man kindly bid him good day and said, "Would you share with a tired old man? I am so very hungry and thirsty."

"I have only stale bread and warm water," Samuel said, "but if you don't mind that, we can eat together."

But when Samuel reached for their snack, he found sweet cake and cider.

"My, look at this," said Samuel.

When they finished their tasty meal, the old man told Samuel, "You shared with me. Now you will have good luck to go with your kind heart."

The man pointed at an old tree nearby. "Cut that tree and you'll find something special there in its trunk." Then the man walked away without another word.

Samuel did as the old man said.

Samuel raised his ax and swiftly cut
down the old tree. When the tree fell, Samuel
found a goose sitting inside its hollow trunk.
Its feathers were made of gold!

Samuel had never seen such a splendid
sight! He picked up the goose and hurried
into town. He had to share this great goose
with everyone he knew.

Samuel beamed proudly as he carried his
golden goose through the town. He passed
an inn, and the innkeeper's three curious
daughters came out to see the beautiful bird.
Each of the three daughters wanted to take
one of the goose's golden feathers to keep for
her own.

When Samuel stopped to show them the goose, the eldest sister tiptoed behind Samuel and tugged at the goose's wing. Her hand stuck there tightly. She waved to her sisters for their help.

The sisters thought that together they could free her. They joined hands to pull. Instead, they found they were all stuck to each other! The sisters scurried behind Samuel, who marched toward the next town with his goose.

Samuel hurried through a field on his way to the next town. The girls followed closely behind. In the field, he passed a minister and his wife.

The minister saw the odd procession and cried out at the sisters, "Have you no shame, girls? Why must you run after the boy?"

The minister tried to pull the youngest girl away. All too soon he felt that he himself was stuck, and he had to run as fast as his legs could carry him to keep up.

The minister's wife saw her husband running along with the three girls. She pulled on his sleeve. Then she was caught up in this silly parade, too.

They passed two farmers on a road. The minister's wife called for help, but as soon as they touched her, the farmers were pulled along, too!

Samuel hurried into the next town, with everyone behind him. There a king lived with his only daughter. The princess was so serious that it was believed she could not laugh. The king proclaimed that whoever made the princess laugh would marry her.

Samuel happened to pass this castle. At the sight of this bumbling parade, the princess burst into fits of laughter.

Samuel asked her to marry him. But the king did not want Samuel to marry his daughter, so he gave him a challenge.

"Bring me a man who can drink a whole cellarful of cider, and eat a mountain of bread," he said, certain Samuel would fail.

Samuel thought of the little man in the woods and rushed off.

"Oh, I'm so thirsty and so very hungry," said the man to Samuel.

Back at the castle, the little man happily drank all the cider and ate all the bread.

But the king had another demand. "Bring me a ship that sails on both land and sea."

Again, Samuel went to see the little man.

"I will share my magic," said the old man, "because you have been so kind to me."

Soon Samuel was back at the castle with a ship that sailed on land and sea. The king had no choice but to let Samuel marry the princess. The two were married that very day.

The Brownie of Blednock

Adapted by Jennifer Boudart
Illustrated by Gwen Connelly

Nighttime was falling over the town of Blednock, and the people who lived there were doing what they did every evening. No one knew it, but something special was about to happen. It all began with a humming noise. The townspeople lined up along Main Street and looked down the road.

They could see somebody coming. People began to whisper to each other. Who was this visitor to Blednock? Why was he humming?

No one had seen a person who looked like this before. The stranger was as small as a boy, but he had a long, brown beard. He wore a tall, pointed hat and tiny, curled-up shoes. He walked closer and closer, and the humming got louder and louder.

That's when they heard what the stranger was humming: "Any work for Aiken-Drum? Any work for Aiken-Drum?"

What was Aiken-Drum? No one seemed to know. The people were more curious than ever. Then Granny, the wisest woman in the town, had something to say. "I think Aiken-Drum is what our visitor calls himself," she announced. "I believe he is a brownie."

BEST-LOVED CHILDREN'S STORIES

Granny shook the brownie's hand, and said, "Speak up, Brownie." So he did.

"The ways of brownies are different from the ways of people," he said. "In our land, we learn to do good by serving others."

The little brownie explained that he was from somewhere far away, and there was not enough work in his land. "I just need a dry place to sleep and something warm to drink at bedtime," said the brownie. In return, he promised to do any kind of work.

"If there's a town that needs a helping hand, it's Blednock," said Granny. She was right. The new church needed building. The old bridge needed mending.

And that is how a brownie came to live in the town of Blednock. All of the townspeople chipped in to try to make the visitor comfortable in his new home.

The blacksmith let Aiken-Drum sleep in a dry corner of his barn. He gave the brownie just a simple horse's blanket to keep warm at night, for that is what Aiken-Drum had requested.

"We brownies don't need anything fancy," Aiken-Drum had reminded him. "A simple blanket from the stable will do."

The blacksmith knew that keeping his sleeping area simple was a way to show respect for Aiken-Drum's wishes.

Every morning, the blacksmith found only an empty mug in the barn and the horse blanket folded neatly in the corner.

Each evening, Granny brought Aiken-Drum plain tea. The rest of the townspeople tried in vain to spot him at work. It always seemed that he was hurrying off to one place or another.

Soon, all of the people of Blednock were sharing stories about his magical work.

"Aiken-Drum fixed a broken wheel on my wagon last night. He must have known I was going to take my grain to the miller today," chuckled Baker Smith. "I am forever grateful to that curious little brownie."

"While I was asleep with fever, Aiken-Drum came," said Mother Jones. "He cleaned my whole house and cooked a big batch of soup!" she said.

"Aiken-Drum brought all my sheep to safety. He took them into the barn just before last night's storm!" said Farmer Adams. "And he did it so quietly, too. I didn't hear a thing until the storm kicked in."

More and more stories were being told of the good work that Aiken-Drum was doing. Wherever work needed to be done, he was there. The town was looking better than it ever had. The new church was even prettier than anyone had hoped.

Aiken-Drum did take breaks from time to time. On still evenings, the brownie sat by the river. He was never alone long. The children of Blednock would come join him.

Children loved Aiken-Drum. He loved them, too. They crowded around, giggling and asking to play this game or that:

"Tell us a story, Aiken-Drum."

"Play hide-and-seek, Aiken-Drum."

Aiken-Drum would start a bonfire and tell stories and play with the children until their parents called them for dinner. When the children went off to their houses, the brownie went off to work. That's the way Aiken-Drum liked it.

Almost everyone thought things around Blednock were better than ever. Only Miss Daisy thought differently. "It's not right for a brownie to work so hard for so little," she said.

Miss Daisy's neighbors shook their heads at her. "Aiken-Drum made it plain," they would say with a sigh. "Brownies work only for the love of making people happy."

Miss Daisy just sniffed. She was sure he needed something more. He simply was too shy to ask. Why, who wouldn't want more than a stable and a horse blanket?

Finally, Miss Daisy decided to do what she thought was best. Everyone would thank her for it later, Aiken-Drum most of all.

One night, Miss Daisy tiptoed into the blacksmith's barn. The brownie wasn't there. Miss Daisy placed a pair of her husband's pants next to his mug.

Well, you can guess what happened. Aiken-Drum took one look at those pants and knew what was happening. Someone had tried to pay him! His new friends had forgotten what mattered most to a brownie, so he disappeared that very night.

The people were heartbroken, and the children saddest of all. But sometimes, when the wind was just right, they could hear faint humming across the river, and they knew their brownie was off helping another town.

The Wild Swans

Adapted by Brian Conway
Illustrated by Kathy Mitchell

nce there was a king who had much
happiness and great fortune. Of all
his treasures, he was proudest of his four
children. His three sons were fine and strong,
and his daughter, Elise, seemed the dearest,
sweetest, and kindest child in all the world.

Then one day the king hurried to find
Elise. "You are in danger," he told her, for he
had wicked enemies who believed no one
should have the happiness the king had.

"I fear for your safety," the king told his daughter. "During the night, your brothers were taken away from us. I know not where. I cannot stand to lose you, too."

The king told the princess to go with his trusted servants, who would take her to safety in their home in the forest.

"When you're old enough," said the king, "find your brothers and come back to me."

He kissed her good-bye. Elise did as her father said. She lived hidden away in the servants' house for many years. She was treated well, but she was very unhappy. Elise longed to see her three beloved brothers and her father again.

When Elise was old enough, she set off to find her brothers. She had no idea where to look, but she had a feeling inside that told her they needed her help.

After several days of wandering, Elise met an old woman at the seashore.

"I am looking for my three brothers," Elise told her. "They are fine, strong princes. Have you seen them?"

"I have seen nothing all day but three white swans with golden crowns on their heads," the old woman said, showing Elise three white feathers. Elise clutched them close to her and fell asleep while she waited for the swans to return.

Just before sunset, Elise woke up to
see three majestic swans gliding down
to the shore. As the last ray of sunshine
disappeared, the three swans changed into
three princes—her brothers! They held her
close and told her what had happened.

Many years ago, an evil sorcerer had
come to the castle. This sorcerer vowed to
ruin the king's happiness, and turned the
three handsome princes into swans. Since
that day, they had lived as swans during
the day and humans during the night.

"We have seen our father," the eldest
brother told Elise. "He serves the sorcerer
against his will."

Elise promised to help free her brothers from the wicked spell. Her brothers told her of an enchanted land far across the sea where they might find a way to break the spell.

"Take me with you," Elise urged them. "I know I can help."

Her brothers crafted a net to carry Elise in. They rushed to reach land by nightfall, or else all three brothers and their sister would drop into the sea.

After two days' flight, they arrived where it was said that the fairy queen lived. Surely she would know how to help them. Elise's brothers found her a cave to rest in while they searched for the fairy queen.

That night, the fairy queen came to Elise in a dream.

"Only you can free your brothers," she told Elise. "But you must sacrifice greatly."

Elise listened carefully.

"Craft a shirt for each brother from rose petals," the fairy queen said. "When you cover the swans with them, the spell will be broken. You may not speak until the shirts are made. If you utter even one word, your brothers will be swans forever."

With that, the fairy queen disappeared. Elise awoke to find the cave surrounded with hundreds of lovely rosebushes. She knew what she had to do.

Elise set to work immediately. She used the roses' prickly thorns as needles to string the petals together. Elise worked tirelessly, day and night. Her brothers visited her, but Elise didn't dare speak.

Soon Elise had but one sleeve left to sew. But that day a woodcutter and his wife came upon Elise's garden. The woodcutter's wife loved roses, and had a lovely garden herself.

"What are you doing out in the woods alone?" she asked, but Elise didn't dare respond. "Poor child, come with us. We'll give you proper food and rest."

Elise did not want to leave the garden. She wanted to finish the third shirt.

Elise gathered up the shirts and as many roses as she could carry.

She stayed with the woodcutter and his wife for many days. At night, she stayed awake to finish the last shirt. But before long, Elise ran out of rose petals.

That night, she creeped out of the house and plucked petals from the garden.

At sunrise, the woodcutter's wife found her in the garden. "Ungrateful girl!" she shouted. "You've ruined my roses!"

At that moment Elise's brothers arrived to visit her. Elise quickly spread the three shirts over the swans.

Before her eyes, the swans became men!

Elise ran to her brothers' arms. Anxious to speak now that the spell had been broken, she explained everything to the woodcutter and his wife. "I'm sorry that I have been so difficult, when you have been so kind," said Elise. "We will repay you."

Elise and her brothers took all of the rosebushes from the forest cave and planted them in the woodcutter's garden.

Then they set off for the sorcerer's castle. The sorcerer was so angered by the spell's failure, he disappeared forever. The king was overjoyed to see his children, and the five set up a new home together in the castle. In the garden, they planted rosebushes.

Ali Baba

Adapted by Brian Conway
Illustrated by Anthony Lewis

In a town in Persia there lived a poor woodcutter called Ali Baba. All he ever wanted was to own a shop, be generous with his neighbors, and have plenty for his family.

One day Ali Baba was cutting wood in the forest. He saw a troop of men on horseback approaching. Ali Baba feared they were robbers, so he climbed a tree to hide.

Ali Baba counted 40 men. Their leader dismounted and stood next to a bush in front of a rock wall. He shouted, "Open, sesame!"

A secret door opened, revealing a cave.

The leader and the other robbers entered
the cave. As they prepared to leave, the leader
closed the door, saying, "Shut, sesame!"
Then the thieves rode away.

When he was sure they were gone,
Ali Baba stepped close and shouted,
"Open, sesame!" And the door opened.

Ali Baba stepped through the doorway
to find a large room filled with all sorts of
valuables made from gold, silver, and jewels.
He feared the robbers might soon return and
quickly gathered as much gold as he could
carry. Now he could finally open his shop!

Ali Baba remembered in his haste to say,
"Shut, sesame!" when he left the cave.

Ali Baba did not notice that he dropped a single gold coin at the base of the bush that covered the secret door.

A few weeks later, the leader caught sight of the coin glimmering in the sunlight. "How could you risk revealing our hiding place?" he asked angrily.

But none of the thieves remembered dropping the coin.

"Then we have been found out," the leader growled. He paced for several minutes with the thieves waiting anxiously for him to speak. Then he announced, "We must learn who is newly rich in the town. That man and all his family must pay."

By now Ali Baba had in fact opened his shop. He was a fair and generous shop owner. He and his family were happy.

Ali Baba hired a helper named Morgiana. She was a very clever and beautiful young lady, and cared for Ali Baba and his family.

One day, a stranger came calling at the shop. He asked Morgiana many questions about the owner. The stranger greatly worried Morgiana.

The disguised thief returned to the cave and said, "The man who found us out is called Ali Baba. He lives behind his new shop in town. He was a poor woodcutter only a few weeks ago."

"Go back there at nightfall," the leader ordered. "Mark his house with this white chalk, and later, we will all go to the marked house and finish him."

One of the robbers moved through the shadows, using his chalk to mark Ali Baba's home. Little did he know that clever Morgiana had spotted him. After the thief marked Ali Baba's door, she followed with her own white chalk and marked the rest of the doors in town.

When the leader and his thieves arrived later that night, they found every door was marked. They did not know which house to attack, so they crept away in shame.

The leader decided to use all his power against Ali Baba. The 40 thieves gathered together and made a plan. The leader would disguise himself as an oil merchant. He would lead a train of mules that carried 39 barrels. The thieves would hide inside the barrels and await the signal. Early that night, the thieves arrived at Ali Baba's shop.

"I have brought some oil to sell at market tomorrow," the leader lied. "But tonight I need a place to stay. Will you take me in?"

Ali Baba was as generous as usual. "Of course you may stay here," he replied. "Leave your cargo in back. There is hay there for the mules. Then come in for dinner."

In the yard, the leader whispered to his men, "Wait until you hear my signal. Then leave your barrels and storm the house."

Later that night, Morgiana was cleaning up when her lamp ran out of oil. Then she remembered the oil barrels out back.

She walked up to a barrel. A voice whispered, "Is it time?"

Morgiana sensed danger. She answered, "Not yet, but soon." Then, gathering some hay around each barrel, Morgiana lit the hay with a torch. The 39 cowardly thieves coughed from the smoke. They popped out from their barrels and ran away to keep from getting burned.

When the leader made his signal, none of his men moved. The next day, he returned to the cave to find his 39 robbers gone. Now on his own, the thief decided he would have to use all his cunning to plan his revenge.

The leader opened a shop across the road from Ali Baba's shop and lived as Cogia Hassan for many months. He waited in this disguise until just the right moment.

After a while, Ali Baba invited the new shop owner over for dinner. Cogia Hassan graciously accepted and brought a basket of fine goods.

But Cogia Hassan carried a dagger in his cloak, intended for Ali Baba and his son.

Morgiana saw the dagger and quickly came up with a plan. She wore long, flowing scarves, then entered the dining room to dance for the guest.

Morgiana danced close to Cogia Hassan. Stepping behind him, Morgiana wrapped the scarf around his arms. He could not move.

"What are you doing?" Ali Baba cried.

"He is your enemy," she explained. "He has a dagger!" Ali Baba's son seized the dagger, and the thief was sent to prison.

"We owe you our lives," Ali Baba said. "Please marry my son and join our family."

Morgiana agreed, and they celebrated with a splendid wedding.

The Nightingale

Adapted by Lisa Harkrader
Illustrated by Robin Moro

any years ago, the emperor of
China lived in a palace surrounded
by beautiful gardens. People traveled from
all over the world to walk the lush paths, and
many claimed that the gardens were the most
beautiful thing in all the world.

One day, a fisherman led some of these
visitors into the forest to see a nightingale
that lived there. When the nightingale
opened its mouth, its voice was pure and
strong. Its song was the most beautiful thing
the visitors had ever heard.

The nightingale became known as the most beautiful thing in China. Soon, everyone had heard of the nightingale. Even the Japanese emperor wanted to see the nightingale, so he sent a letter to the emperor of China telling him that he planned to visit in two days' time.

The emperor summoned his prime minister. "The emperor of Japan will arrive soon," said the emperor. "He expects to see this nightingale. Search until you find it."

The emperor's servants searched the gardens for two full days until they found the nightingale. The bird was very plain, but its song was very beautiful.

When the emperor of Japan arrived, he was taken to the nightingale right away. "So this is the most beautiful thing in all of China," said the emperor of Japan. "I must say, it looks rather plain. How could such a lovely song come from this dull little bird?"

Just then, the nightingale sang, and the emperor of Japan was speechless. It was the most beautiful sound he had ever heard.

The emperor of China loved the bird's song, but he too wished that the nightingale was more beautiful. So the emperor of China placed the bird in a golden cage and adorned its feathers with jewels and satin ribbons. Inside its gilded cage, the bird was beautiful.

One day a gift arrived from the emperor of Japan. "This is a small token compared with the joy your bird gave me," he wrote.

The gift was a replica of the nightingale, encrusted with emeralds and rubies. On its back was a silver key. When the emperor wound the key, the mechanical bird sang a simple song. The replica couldn't sing like the nightingale, but it was beautiful.

The emperor put the replica in a golden cage next to the nightingale and wound its key. When the replica began to sing, the nightingale stopped its song.

The next day, the emperor could not find the nightingale. The bird had flown away.

One day, missing the nightingale, the emperor wound up the replica and the mechanical bird sang. Suddenly, with a loud pop and a twang, the bird stopped.

No one was able to fix the replica or find the emperor's beloved nightingale. Over time, the emperor missed the nightingale's song so much that he became very ill.

One morning the nightingale returned, and sang its beautiful song. The emperor was so pleased that he began to feel much better.

The emperor told the nightingale that its song was more beautiful and precious to him than any sparkling jewel. From that day on, the nightingale never left the emperor's side.

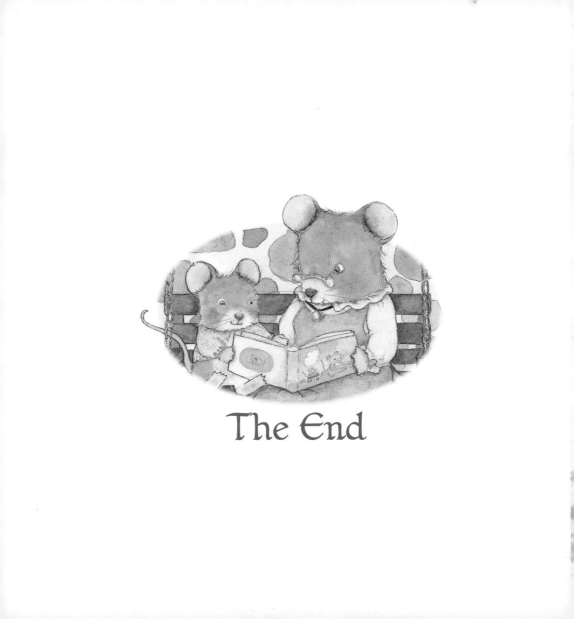

The End